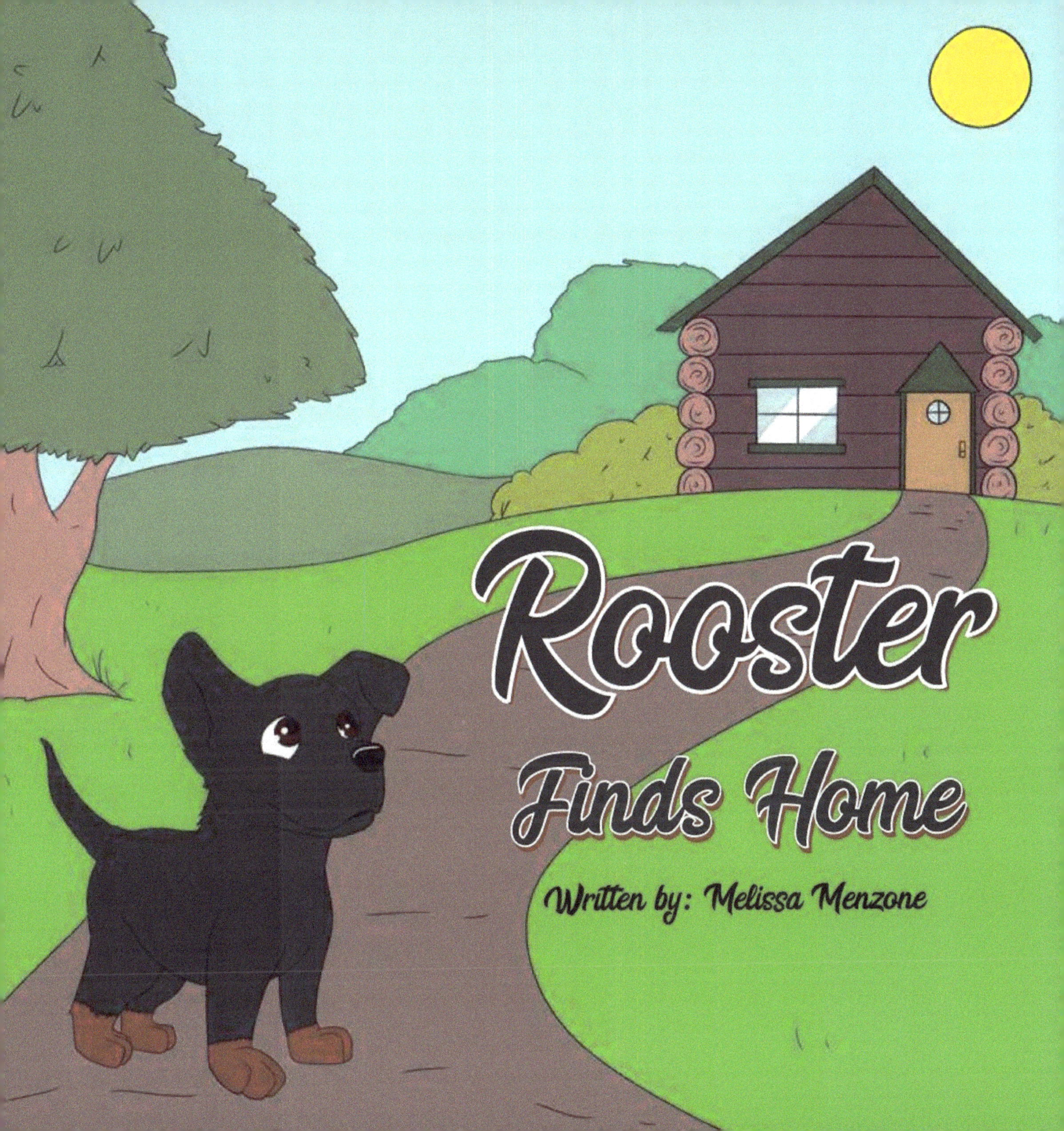

Rooster
Finds Home
Written by: Melissa Menzone

Silver Pencil Press

Hi! My name is Rooster and I'm a puppy.

One day when I was really little, my mother took my four sisters, my brother, and me out of our box in the shed to see the yard. It was exciting! She led us along on a path in some long, green grass. I was so short I couldn't see over the grass, but boy did it smell good, everything smelled so fresh and airy.

Mother showed us a tree and brought us to a large flat rock heated by the sun. There she lined us up and told us about the world. She said, "One day all my little puppies will leave here to find a home."

I didn't believe that. I was happy here. And then, we all curled up for a nap on that warm sunny stone.

The others were still sprawled in the sun when I awoke, so I wriggled my way off the rock to investigate the nearby bushes. The leaves were big and heavy and the stems were spiny. But I could smell something tempting hiding behind them. I pushed up into the bush and found raspberries – a treat just for me!

I struggled, balancing on my back legs and waving my front paws, before I managed to catch a ripe, red raspberry. It was so sweet and delicious! But I couldn't just have one, so I started tugging at the branches to get more.

I'd managed to get another berry when all of a sudden, my mother barked, "No, puppy!" The berry tumbled onto the ground.

My mother dashed off the rock startling my sleepy sisters and brother and grabbed me by the scruff of my neck. I stepped on the fallen berry when trying to keep up with her as she pulled me away from the bushes. "Those raspberries belong to the farmer. He'll be really angry if we take them," she said.

"I'm sorry, Mother," I replied tucking my nose to my chest.

"Remember, only good puppies find nice homes," she instructed.

Meanwhile, one of my sisters leapt past us and greedily snatched up the crushed berry. Two other sisters pounced on her, squabbling over who would get the berry. My last sister and my brother sniffed around the bushes, jumping to reach the fruit.

I knew better than to disobey my mother. So I sat there watching the frolicking and wishing I could join the fun. Mother was rather angry at the antics.

"No. No puppies," my mother growled, calling my siblings to attention. "We must go back to the shed. Playtime is over," she added. Using her nose, she pushed all of us away from the raspberries.

Just then, a loud, scary noise boomed overhead. I jumped and then buried my head in the long grass with my eyes squeezed shut.

"Run puppies! Run for our box!" my mother shouted and I heard my sisters and brother scrambling in the grass and over the flat stone, but I was so scared I didn't move.

The ground started trembling beneath a great roar and I heard a man, the farmer, yelling, "Catch those dogs! I'll teach them a lesson for digging in my garden!"

Scared or not, I took my mother's advice and ran!

I remembered our box in the shed. It was nearby, over a small hill, past a big tree, through a gravel yard. But no matter how far I ran, I couldn't find the shed. I climbed many hills, up one side and down the other. I found trees, lots of them growing close together with shrubs and thorn bushes around their base. But nowhere did I find a shed.

I wandered nervously down a leaf-strewn path in the woods. Nothing smelled, sounded, or looked familiar. I stopped at a nest of birds, a dozen tall brown birds and asked them for directions back to my mother.

"We're turkeys, puppy! What do we know about boxes?" the biggest of them said.

"Your nests look warm, can I stay with you?" I asked.
Several turkeys stood, fanning their feathers. The big one jabbed at me with his large beak. "Be away, now, puppy!" he cackled, flapping his big wings. The other turkeys joined with hisses.

I turned and ran.

It was getting dark and my stomach growled. Mother always fed us in the grey light of evening. "Mother!" I called into the blackness settling around me, "Mother!" but she never answered me.

I remembered her lesson, "all puppies leave to find a home." Was this what she meant? Did home mean being alone and unhappy?

I found a hole between two stones filled with dead leaves and squirmed my way inside. I was so tired that my legs shook. So scared that my heart pounded and I jerked at every strange noise. In the dark of night there were a lot of frightening sounds. I closed my eyes and cried for my mother.

In the morning, I found the wood filled with birds and squirrels and chipmunks, all happily passing by my little hole. I was miserable as I started on my way. I followed the sunlight, calling for my mother, hoping to find the shed.

It was a long walk and the bottoms of my paws hurt. But then the trees gave way to a grass filled yard and a house. Suddenly I remembered – house meant home! A warm sunny porch beckoned me as I ran across the soft grass. And a bowl of water sat next to the front door!

I drank every drop of water and wished for more. No one came to the door, though, when I called. So I spread myself out on the warm boards and examined my aching feet. It took several hours to pull thorns out of my paws and clean my wounds.

Everything was so peaceful here.

I was just falling asleep when a woman screamed, "Argh!"

Next thing I saw were two skinny legs in black tights and a straw broom hurtling towards me. "Get out, you dirty, mangy thing! Go away!" the woman hollered, swinging the broom menacingly.

I bolted to my feet, scurried backwards as fast as I could, and tumbled right off the porch landing in a prickly evergreen bush. The woman whacked her broom against the bush. Thankfully she didn't hit me, but I knew enough not to stay any longer and once again found myself wandering in the woods.

Apparently, not all houses meant home.

I dreaded spending another night away from my sisters and brother. I wanted my mother. I wandered with tears in my eyes, my throat hoarse from crying, "Mother!" not paying any attention to where my feet went when something jumped out of a bush right behind me.

"Howdy, puppy! What's up with you?"

I tripped over my own feet, spinning and falling into a ball beneath a tall, long, sort of plump, but scruffy looking, cat.

"Custer's my name," he purred, flexing the claws on his front paws. "You lost, puppy?"

I tried to explain everything that happened, but Custer didn't seem to understand, or care. "I'm not your friend, puppy," he said when I'd finished then shook his fur and trotted away. I scurried after him. He moved fast and seemed to know exactly where he was going. I was panting heavily trying to keep up.

"Still following me?" Custer asked after a while. He sat in a sunny spot and began pruning himself. I plopped down on the ground beside him.

"I had a home once but I like my freedom better," Custer said. "I'm not ever going back." He grabbed at his own belly with his teeth and spit out a fur ball. "Nasty ticks! I tell you, puppy, stay in the wood for long and ticks and fleas will get you."

I put my nose out to the fur ball, but didn't want to get too close. It smelled nasty. Satisfied, Custer stretched and began trotting away, but not before stating, "Listen, I'll feed you supper, but that's all. I've got myself to protect."

Custer didn't go far. He stopped at the edge of a wide brook. Mother had told us stories about swimming and I have to admit the water looked exciting. I moved closer to the edge, trying to reach the white foam gathering and spinning off in pieces around boulders or see what made the ripples sparkle. But Custer hissed at me to keep back, "Out of the way, puppy, unless you want to starve!"

Long, skinny, silver fish wasn't the best meal I'd ever had. The pieces Custer threw at me had too many bones and the skin was rubbery, hard to chew. I gnawed at it though, grateful for something to eat.

"I've seen your kind eating them blueberries, puppy," Custer remarked, licking his lips and paws. He paused long enough to point out a clump of bushes. "Go on, try 'em. Too sweet for me; they hurt my teeth."

Blueberries are even better than raspberries! But a lot more work to pull them from the bushes. After filling myself with too many blueberries, I turned back to Custer to ask where we'd sleep.

Custer was gone. Night had come. I looked around, terrified, trying to find somewhere to hide. I was alone, again. I called for my sisters and brother, again. I cried, "Mother!" again.

No one came, but those strange, nighttime wood noises grew louder. I crawled under some dead leaves, thinking about ticks and cats, brooms and turkeys, and cried myself to sleep, again.

There was no sun the following morning and I was depressed. I ate some more blueberries, but even their sweet juice didn't boost my cheer. I called for my mother. I called for Custer. Several squirrels chirped at me. The water gurgled. And some heavy wind noise came from beyond the trees.

Sticking my nose out to smell danger, I inched my way towards the wind noise. One moment I was creeping through heavy woods and the next I was on a strip of grass alongside a long black ribbon. It was a road!

The brook rushed under a bridge and cars swooped by at a dizzying speed, sending strong gusts of wind into the woods.

Mother always warned us puppies: "Stay away from the road!" Our shed was next to the road. My heart leapt and I trotted along the road edge first left and then right, looking for the shed. "Mother!" I called as loud as I could over the car noise.

But I still couldn't see the shed.

Before long, one of those cars pulled over to the side of the road. Scared, I backed into a bush and tried to hide beneath its low branches. I was cold and tired and hungry, again. I trembled beneath that bush, watching two big feet circle around the front of that huge car.

"Well, what have we here?" a man asked. He crouched down in front of my bush. He had big brown eyes, just like my mother! And he smiled. "Are you lost, little puppy?"

The man put out his hand, but didn't move any closer. I stared at him crouching there. He was a policeman. I crawled forward, but I was still scared. Policeman. Stranger. Policeman. Mother always said to be careful of strangers. But policemen were supposed to help and this man seemed so friendly.

"Come, little puppy," the policeman said. He had big, warm hands and he picked me up gently.

"You're shivering. And, I bet you're hungry!" He tucked me against his chest. I rested my head on his shoulder.

"Nothing to do but take you home," he said, patting my head.

I was so relieved that I started crying.

HOME. Mother told the most wonderful stories about HOME. She'd said nice people would love me. Nice people would feed me and play with me. Nice people would raise me to be a great dog.

I snuggled closer to this big, warm, friendly policeman and licked his chin.

"My name is David," the policeman said. "What's yours?"

Today I live in a big HOME made of logs with a porch in front and a deck out back. I still miss my mother and my sisters and my brother. But now I have Daddy David and Mummy Millie who take care of me.

They gave me this grand name, too: Rooster!

I am the luckiest puppy in the world!

Rooster Finds Home
Talking Points for Teachers and Parents

Dear Teacher or Parent,

You know your children better than I, but I had hoped that this story would teach children three important, life-long lessons. I've listed them here for your consideration. Thank you for including Rooster's journey home in your children's upraising.

Respectfully,

Melissa

Talking Point 1: Why does Rooster run away from the turkeys? Many children feel ashamed or embarrassed because they are different from the other children in their class or neighborhood. Differences come from illness, deformities, skin color, or religious creed. Children should be aware that we are all different and mocking someone's differences shouldn't be tolerated.

Talking Point 2: What can excessive fear and loneliness lead to in children? Many children lose a parent or guardian early in life, as Rooster did. Many others are born never knowing their parents. Sadness such as this can lead to depression and a desire to stay away from life. Children should be willing to comfort their young friends who might suddenly be crying and wanting to be alone.

Talking Point 3: Why does Rooster feel attracted to Policeman David? It's not just about the authority and security, although respecting authority (police, teachers, parents) is an extremely important lesson. Children need to understand that they can't bully their playmates into being friends. Bullying causes resentment in the other children. Genuine kindness will forge a longer-lasting, loyal, relationship and will be much rewarded.

Other Talking Points include: Why was Rooster's mother upset when she found him eating the raspberries? (stealing someone's livelihood) What is the difference between eating the raspberries and eating the blueberries? (survival in the wilderness) Why would Custer the Cat want to help a puppy? (perception, not all "natural enemies" are in fact enemies) Why did Rooster feel disappointed after Custer disappeared? And, why should children persevere even though they are sad, lonely, frightened, or disappointed? Life is difficult, but it is worth living.

Also Available

Rooster Encuentra su Hogar

Rooster Goes Camping

Rooster's Day at the Spa

Rooster's Playtime

Rooster's Playtime 2